LOCKED UP FOR BAD BEHAVIOR

Hucow Milking Story

Leandra Camilli

CONTENTS

Title Page

Copyright

Chapter 1 — 1

Chapter 2 — 5

Chapter 3 — 8

Chapter 4 — 12

Chapter 5 — 15

Epilogue — 18

Teaser: Handcuffed for Bad Behavior — 21

Similar Books — 25

About the Author — 27

CHAPTER 1

What was I even doing in this place? I asked myself, opening my eyes and realizing that I was somewhere completely different. But then, it dawned on me. I had finally gotten here. I was in Deimour College, the place where they were going to teach me how to become a hucow.

My heart was already tight and excited just thinking about it.

I was on a bed and it was dark, and the mattress was a little cold, but it was nothing that could make me think that I had made a mistake coming here. Quite the opposite, in fact. I thought something differently about it.

As soon as I had opened my eyes, I realized that I couldn't see anything, and it was much graver than that. I also felt like I couldn't feel anything. I felt like I couldn't feel my legs, my arms, and even my pussy.

But that didn't make any sense. I could feel my pussy, and I knew that it was between my legs, just waiting to be played with. That was why I didn't stop myself before lowering my hand and finding it.

I gave it a little rub, making me moan in the darkness of the room. I should be thinking that there was probably someone watching me doing this, and I was, but instead of that deterring me from going on with this, it was actually spurring me to do the opposite.

I flicked my finger over my pussy again, focusing on my clit. As soon as I did that, I moaned again, my body trembling in pleasure.

I had never felt so much pleasure in my life. There was

something different about touching myself in the darkness and when I was completely alone, like now.

I took a deep breath in, checking my surroundings to make sure that no cameras were recording this. But it was pointless. Even if cameras were recording me, I wouldn't be able to make them out in the dark.

I took another deep breath, my finger flicking over my pussy and clit, over and over, and this time I was growing bolder.

I couldn't help but wonder what they would do after finding me doing this. They would certainly lock me up for bad behavior, and that wouldn't even be the beginning of it. I was certain of it.

I took another deep breath, noticing how sweaty my skin was getting. A moment later, I was picking up the pace. My finger was rubbing, enticing, grazing, and doing all other sorts of things to my needy snatch, and I couldn't stop myself anymore.

I was so certain of that I knew I was going to come and when I did, it would be like I had the first and best orgasm of my life.

I would feel like a man had finally penetrated me for the first time, and I would be breathless, my body trembling for hours on end.

I felt like my world was going to explode when the door opened and a man stepped in. I should stop what I was doing, but seeing him stepping through the door was making me do the opposite.

I increased my pace, my finger fucking, touching, and doing other indescribable things to my clit. My body was getting so hot that I was soaking the bedsheets, and that just didn't happen often, not even when I was inspired.

I couldn't see his face, but I could tell that he had a strong, well-defined jawline, short hair, and was even married.

I knew that he was one of the teachers of the college, a thought that sent me into overdrive. The fact that he was here and seeing me like this, checking me out, meant that he thought I was hot enough to be his protégé.

Or something along those lines.

And looking down, even though where the light was coming

from mostly hid his bulge, I could tell that he was hard. After all, I could see the outline of his prick poking against his pants, and that made me feel so much like putting his dick between my lips.

I couldn't help but wonder how I would feel when he was pounding in and out of me.

Finally penetrating me.

Going all the way in.

Doing things to me I never even thought possible. And I was certain he was thinking the same thing as well. So certain that I couldn't stop brushing and flicking my finger over my clit, as though it was the last thing I was doing with my life.

He stepped toward me and now I could see his face better. It was still not enough, but I could make out some of the features. He really was handsome and my type of guy.

I wondered if he knew that and if he was going to use that information to his advantage.

It was coming.

My orgasm was coming and there was nothing I could do about it. I had no more control over my hand, and my fingers were moving on their own. I could feel my body getting hotter as time passed, and I could also feel my orgasm coming, and when it did, I knew that it would shower my body with it.

In the meantime, that guy was just standing there, watching me as though I was some kind of animal trapped in a cell.

"You should be locked up. I thought that I was going to come here and see someone that could behave a little better sometimes, but I'm seeing the exact opposite right now. You're not allowed to touch yourself like that."

What he just said was supposed to make me stop, but it did the exact opposite. My finger moved faster, flicking over and over my pussy, my pussy lips, and my clit, and before long I was arching my back.

That was it. My climax, and it was as destructive, everlasting, and explosive as I'd thought. I moaned a lot louder than I thought I ever could, and when I was done, I could still feel the aftershocks traveling in my body.

I then looked up, finding his eyes, and I noticed that the man was standing much closer to me. I couldn't believe what he had just said to me, and I couldn't believe that I knew it was going to lead to a punishment I never thought possible.

CHAPTER 2

He grabbed my hand and took me from there without doing anything that resembled if he felt any pity for me. It was the exact opposite of that. He dragged me over the floor, down the hallway, and I couldn't help but notice that my boobs were grazing over the floor. It hurt me, but it was good. So good that I didn't want it to end at all.

He took me over to one of the cells in the college. The college looked like a castle. The walls were thick, cold, and the place itself stood on a huge island, and from here we could see the continent and the people that lived there, not giving as much as a thought about what was going on here.

He put me in that cell and then walked inside, locking the door behind him. It was still dark, but the lighting in the cell was better than it was in that room with the bed.

I could see his face better now, and I couldn't help but think that he really was my type of man. Everything about him resonated with me, and it wasn't just his rippling muscles, his massive bulge, his thick legs, and pretty much everything else about him that made me feel that way about this.

His eyes checked me from bottom to top, and I was on the floor, sitting on it.

And without any further complications, his fingers started to unbuckle his belt. Oh, he really was going to do it? I didn't even have to ask that. It was more than obvious that he was, given the way that he was 'eating' me with his eyes.

"You really want to see my cock, don't you, bitch?" He asked me, brushing his fingers over my forehead.

"I want to see your big cock, master. I want to feel it in my mouth, between my lips, down in my throat, and doing so many other things. I know that you can make all of that real to me."

"That's my plan, baby girl," he said, finishing unbuckling his belt and then letting his professor pants fall to the floor, finally revealing for the delight of my eyes his massive, meaty, impressive, thick cock.

I gasped just looking at it. There was a bead of pre-come coming through the slit, and I couldn't help but wonder if it would be possible to lick it with my tongue.

I was certain he was thinking the same thing as well, wasn't he?

He put his fingers around his massive dong, moving the skin up and down as if he was trying to tease me. If that was the case, it was working.

I was doing everything in my power not to come crashing down with my head, wrapping my lips around his prick, and then giving him the blowjob of his life.

I was certain he would appreciate that, and also everything else I could do with my tongue...

But I was only going to do that when I had his command.

He slapped my face, making the skin sting. Wow. I didn't think he was just going to do that. He did it without warning me, and it hurt, but I wasn't going to hate him for it.

It was the opposite. I could feel my pussy getting wetter after that slap.

"You do everything as I say, and you can only do everything I say to you. I *own* you. I'm your master, and that will never change. It doesn't matter how much the other guys want you as well, you are always going to be mine and entirely mine."

"But I'm so naughty and my boobs feel so sore. I think that I'm already becoming a hucow even though they haven't started my transformation yet."

He slapped my face again. It stung just like the first time, and I didn't think he was going to do it again. In the meantime, my eyes couldn't stop diverting to his cock dangling between his legs. It was already hard. I could see the veins snaking on it, and I couldn't help but wonder how I would feel when I had my fingers wrapped around it.

"You can be as naughty as you want, but you are always going to do everything I want, and when I'm not around and one of the guys shows up, asking you to be with them, you are going to say no, you understand me?" He asked me, his eyes glaring at me and I felt like he was burning my soul with that stare.

I nodded, putting my fingers under my boobs, pressing them up, and showing him how willing I was. He liked that, I could tell. He liked that so much that he wanted to be with his lips wrapped around my nipples, and I was certain he was going to do that as soon as I finished giving him a blowjob.

"I'm going to do everything and the only things you want, master," I promised and he smiled after seeing the obedience on my face. I was always going to be obedient to my master.

I was always going to be obedient to Jason, and even though I had to come here to learn how to be a hucow so that I could be sold later, I was going to stay for the sex.

He brushed his fingers under my chin and I heard him purring, showing how content he was with my answer. "Good girl. I knew you were going to say the right thing. And now that you've said it, it's time you showed me what you can do with your mouth when it's on my cock."

Finally.

It was going to happen and my heart was beating so fast while I kept on thinking about how I was going to do this.

And... Should I say that I was a virgin?

CHAPTER 3

It wasn't like Jason couldn't or wouldn't find out the truth, anyway. The way he was looking at me, it was obvious that he was getting suspicious about it. He slapped my face again, and I loved it. I wanted him to keep slapping my face like this for hours on end, and I was certain that he was thinking the same thing.

I could feel the welt on my cheek, and I looked down at his cock again. Then, I looked up, finding his eyes. My eyes were like two little beads asking for his permission so that I could do what I wanted.

Then, Jason nodded, and I was overjoyed. He gave me the permission I needed to suck him off, and I couldn't have asked for anything better.

My fingers were trembling, but the moment that he withdrew his hand, I knew that I had the opportunity I was looking for.

My throat was dry. His cock was pointing at my face, and I noticed, after going on my knees, that I was level with it. It looked threatening and so mean that I didn't know if I would be doing the right thing by putting it in my mouth, but I also knew that I was only thinking things that didn't exist.

I started to lower and lift the skin of his prick, revealing the cockhead and then hiding it, and then again and again, and until I was more comfortable with it. When I was, he started to moan and groan, closing his eyes slightly.

Everything was so dark and I couldn't help but wonder what was happening with the other hucows that were in the other cells.

Could they hear this? I didn't know, but I didn't care either.

What I cared about was that I was having the moment of my life with my master, and I was finally on the verge of making this dream a reality.

Putting his cock into my mouth.

And I could also see his balls and how they moved with the movement of my hand. They hung so low and looked so big - bigger than any other nuts I had seen in my life. They were also so tempting that I just wanted to be playing with them as well, but only if I had his permission.

Then, as if to show me that he was getting tired of my pace, he clamped his hand on my head, shoving it down, and it happened so fast that I didn't have enough time to react.

One moment I was with my hand stroking his dick, and the next his cockhead was penetrating my mouth without showing a shred of mercy. It was absolutely devastating, but also so lovely and such a huge turn-on, too.

It was bliss. Having his dick in my mouth, going all the way down, until I couldn't feel anything else in my throat that wasn't it. And it stretched my lips beyond any level I thought possible, and it started to hurt me, but it wasn't enough to make me regret my decision.

I was just so overjoyed that I was finally giving him head and then I was making him so happy. After looking up, I noticed the smile on Jason's face, and that this time he had reopened his eyes, looking down at me.

I could also see his legs and how hairy they were. Since I couldn't use my hands to please and worship his cock anymore, I decided to use them for something else. I started to massage and knead the skin of his thick, hairy legs with them, and I could feel as though my body was becoming one with this.

Now that his cock was all the way down in my throat, I could start to focus on something else, and that was bobbing my head up and down, especially so that I was pleasing him as much as I could.

And I was.

I didn't have any experience other than from the times when I sucked off bananas, but this was still working, and I knew more or less how to wipe my tongue over his prick, over his cockhead, focusing on the parts where he felt more pleasure and his body trembled more, and it was without a shred of a doubt absolutely mesmerizing.

If we didn't stop this now, I knew that he would be coming into my mouth, and that was everything I wanted at this moment.

I wanted his prick coming inside my mouth, and I knew that it was going to happen. My heart was tight thinking about it.

A moment later, I increased my pace, swiping my tongue over his cockhead, over and over again, rubbing it under his gland, moving my head up and down, and this was all happening for what felt like an eternity, and I noticed how hot my body was getting, and I just wanted this to last as long as possible, even though, given the way that he kept on moaning and groaning so much louder than before, I knew that it wasn't possible.

"I'm going to come, baby. I'm going to come in your mouth, and then, after this, I'm going to come in your pussy too, and the next thing you will say to me is that you are pleased that I was the one that got you pregnant."

I couldn't do anything other than mumble over and over again, but I still knew that he was aware of what I had just said. I was thinking that he thought I was worth it.

He thought I was worth having his seed in my belly, and if there was something that I wanted to do here, other than my first milking, it was to get pregnant.

And if he was to become the bull father of my calf, then all the better. It was such a huge turn-on that it was almost like a kink.

Then, he finally came inside my mouth and cleaned up after himself, which was a pity. I was hoping that he was going to let me clean the mess that we'd made with my tongue, but in the end, it wasn't meant to be.

He turned around, closed the door of the cell after stepping out of it, and then he looked at me as though he wanted to eat me alive.

"I'm going to come back, but until then, you are not allowed to touch yourself again. You are not allowed to do the things we did together but with another guy. I know that some of the teachers here have been talking about you, and they can't have you. I don't like sharing."

I couldn't do anything other than nod.

It was a sign of my submission to him and he was happy with it.

CHAPTER 4

But it wasn't like making that happen was easy. I was walking outside of the room where I slept. I didn't know if this was the reason why it happened, but after I sucked off Jason, they put me back in my bedroom, and it was like torture. In my bedroom, I had privacy and whenever I had privacy, I felt like touching myself.

But I was certain that there were cameras in the room recording me, thus I couldn't touch myself, which was like torture.

That was why I didn't feel like being in my bedroom, even though I could.

For the time being, I wasn't thinking about anything in particular, and I was just strolling down the hallway, eventually turning at a corner when I felt a hand pushing against my chest and then onto a wall of the hallway.

I looked up and I found none other than another of the teachers, and he was staring into my eyes as though he wanted to eat me alive.

I didn't know his name, but that didn't last long until I flicked my eyes down, finding his name on the pin on his chest. His name was Stephen and he was like a God. So tall, so imposing, and so dominating as well.

The mere fact that he was pushing me against a wall made me melt. I couldn't do anything. I couldn't fight against his urges, and I knew that he wanted to do something with me and that it would leave Jason pissed if he found out.

"What's a pretty girl like you doing here, walking around here without even looking where you're going?" He asked, nearing his head to mine, and I thought he was going to kiss me, but he didn't.

He was such a tease, pretty much like everyone else here in the college, except for Jason, who was more like a hands-on kind of guy.

"I was just exploring the place. I'm pretty new here, and I wanted to know what it's like on the inside so that I'm better used to the fact that I'm going to be living here for a while."

He blinked twice, and I was certain that he didn't believe what I had just said. His fingers started to move up and then he found my shoulders, moving them down, and, in less than a moment, his fingers started to tease my nipple. My right nipple, I noticed.

I was already a complete, transformed hucow, and I knew that his hormones were flaring. After giving a glance down, I was so certain of that because I could see the outline of his hard, enraged prick under his pants, and it was as threatening as Jason's.

"You are so big, master. Do you want to be my master as well? Jason… He left me completely alone, promised me that he was going to come back for more, but then he didn't, and now I feel so disappointed."

I knew that I was crossing a line, saying something that I shouldn't, but it didn't matter anyway. What I wanted to do was to find out how big he was, and I knew he was also thinking the same thing. I was so certain of that it wasn't surprising when he grabbed one of my udders, lifting it and then putting the nipple into his mouth.

Oh fuck, he was going to start to suck my milk out of my udder, and that thought alone was enough to make me feel shockwaves of pleasure traveling in my body. If before I felt like it had melted, now it was even worse.

His fingers pressed into my udder.

His lips applied pressure around my nipple, which was big enough for his lips.

Then, he closed his eyes as I started to squirt out line after line of my milk inside his mouth, and it was unbelievably rewarding. I hadn't felt like this in such a long time, and still, it wasn't enough.

I needed more.

I needed everything else that he could give me, thus it wasn't surprising when he lowered his hand, cupping my snatch.

He started to rub it on it, driving me wild, and I shut my eyes, grinding my body against his. Since he was a teacher, he was still dressed, which was a pity for me.

Minutes later, he finally lowered his pants, and now I knew that I had what I was looking for.

I glanced down, finding his prick, and noticed that it was pointing right at me. It was so big, but even though I wanted to be with my mouth all over it, it still wouldn't be enough.

I wanted something else, something that he could give me, and that was him pushing past my pussy lips, stretching me beyond imagination, and then pounding in and out of me like I was nothing.

Finding his eyes, I knew that was exactly what he was thinking at the moment.

CHAPTER 5

He pushed me down until I was lying on the floor, his fingers stroking his massive prick. It wasn't long until he said, "Turn around, on your knees, and show me your ass. I'm going to take your virginity, and it's going to happen right at this moment."

The moment he said that, I obeyed him. I turned around, went on my knees, and then lifted my ass so that it was pointed at his prick. He smiled, went down on his knees as well, and then started to finger my pussy, making me moan and groan, shockwaves of pleasure traveling in my body.

Was he really finally going to penetrate me?

I didn't know, but my body was more than ready for it, and I just wanted that to happen. Thus, it was unsurprising when he grabbed me by putting both of his hands on my shoulders, and then he pulled me back, pushing past my entrance.

Just when that was happening, we noticed that footsteps were approaching us from behind him. I knew that it had to be another teacher, but I had no idea who he was, and he might be Jason, too.

In case he was, my heart would be so tight I would feel like I was going to have a heart attack.

Then, the footsteps stopped the moment when Stephen stopped pushing inside of me, which was a pity. I had to grit my teeth, bite my bottom lip, and do everything possible so that I didn't scream much, but it was still not enough.

"I told you that you weren't supposed to do the things we did together but with another guy. I'm so disappointed in you, Ann,"

Jason said, and I knew that it was his voice. I knew it so well that it sent ripples of fear in my mind, and my body froze up.

I thought that Stephen was just going to pull out of me right away, but he didn't. He stood where he was, with his cockhead pressing against my hymen, and I wondered if and when he was finally going to take my virginity like he'd promised.

"Jason?" He asked, looking over his shoulder and smiling devilishly. I'd thought that he was going to feel some remorse, maybe even some fear for the fact that he was caught red-handed, but he didn't. In fact, it was the opposite. He was daring Jason into a fight with him, and I was certain that was something he just wasn't going to do.

They could both have me, and I could have a lot more than just losing my virginity.

"Yeah, it's me. She is mine. You can't be the one to take her virginity," he growled and I really thought that they were going to start fighting against each other, but they didn't.

I didn't know what they were talking through their stares, but I knew that they were making some kind of agreement.

Then, it finally made sense to me. Stephen pulled out rather unceremoniously, and then he said, "I suppose that you should be the one to do it, then, especially because you are the one that found her and brought her here to become the hucow that she is."

I couldn't see what was happening behind me, but I knew that Jason was smirking. "That's right. I was the one that found her, and I'm the one that has all the rights over her."

I should be feeling pissed that that was what he was talking about me, but I felt the opposite. I felt my nipples so hard and milk coming out of them and down on the floor of the hallway. And in the meantime, I couldn't help but wonder when they were finally going to milk me dry.

And I didn't have to wonder much longer. Stephen, who was looking disappointed that he wasn't going to be the one to take my virginity, stepped so that he was standing in front of me.

Then, he got under me and put my left nipple inside his mouth. He started to suck on it, applying pressure, and the way that he closed his eyes and focused only on what he was doing, showed me how much he was enjoying this.

Then, I felt a pair of hands grabbing my waist, pulling me back slightly, and then I noticed that Jason was lowering his pants. The moment he did that, he got down on his knees, pressed his cockhead against my entrance, and then he began to nudge it until he felt comfortable enough to impale me.

When he did that, I felt more pleasure and pain than ever before in my life, and I was certain that he was even bigger than Stephen, a fact that I decided to keep to myself.

"Jesus, you are so tight and warm," he said, going all the way inside of me, penetrating me much deeper than I ever thought possible, and then he started to roll his hips, finding my G spot, thrusting, fucking me, and eating me raw. I couldn't even breathe properly, and sweat started to cover my entire skin.

Everything was bliss, and then I noticed that my left udder was already drying up. I looked down and I noticed that Stephen was far from satisfied with that. He needed more, and he was going to get it.

Without warning me, he moved to the right, putting my right nipple between his lips again. The moment he did that, he started to suck on it again, and from then on it was only pleasure and pain at the same time. But the pain started to subside, and that meant I could enjoy this as much as I already was.

I had to do something and I knew what that was so that I could reach my orgasm as well.

EPILOGUE

Jason was still inside of me, and it was the most liberating thing that ever happened to me. He was absolutely ruthless, pounding in and out of me, thrusting in and out, ravaging my snatch beyond anything I thought possible. He just wouldn't stop, and that thought never even crossed his mind, and I doubted it ever would.

In the meantime, I was doing everything in my power so that I didn't feel overwhelmed. My body was resonating with this, and I was barely aware that Stephen was under me, with my nipple still inside his mouth, and sucking on it as much as he could and for as long as possible.

His face was the very definition of bliss, and I was feeling so much pleasure that I was drooling from both sides of my mouth.

It was something that never happened to me, even when I was so horny that I could come in less than a couple of seconds.

Some moments later, Jason started to erupt inside of me, getting me pregnant. He was knocking me up, and that thought sent me into overdrive. I didn't even have to start flicking, rubbing, and enticing my clit with my finger so that I came as well. It just happened naturally and before long, I was huffing and feeling the aftershocks of my orgasm.

It was devastating, but very much rewarding as well. By the time it was over, I knew that this was far from finished. I knew that because even though Stephen wasn't the one that took my virginity, he still wanted to pound me with his massive prick, and I was just waiting for that to happen.

It was with that thought in mind that I felt Jason pulling out with a low groan. Then, he stepped so that he was in front of me and his cock was pointed at my mouth. I wondered what he was going to do with it, but I didn't have to be doing that for much longer.

No more than a second later, he pried open my mouth with his fingers, and then inserted his prick between my lips, making me feel more pleasure than before.

I was still huffing and having difficulty breathing, but it was okay. What mattered was that he was going to let me give him another blowjob, and that was exactly what I wanted.

In no time at all, I started to bob up and down on his prick, enjoying every moment of this, and it was like it was going to last for all of eternity.

In the meantime, I could feel Stephen penetrating me. He went all the way inside, found my G spot, and then started to rub against it, and I couldn't help but move my body as he did, following his rhythm, matching him thrust for thrust, and then I came another time, and then one more time, and by the time I stopped coming, I felt like I was going to pass out.

I only didn't because Jason's dong was in my mouth, and he was already getting tired of the way I was moving my head up and down on it.

He grabbed my hair, slapped my face without as much as showing an ounce of remorse, and then he started to shove my head up and down, making me fuck his dick as much as it was ravaging my throat, and it was so much better than everything I ever wanted.

Seconds later, his cock started to erupt inside my mouth, and it began to shoot out rope after rope of his delicious come all over my tongue, making me go wild. His milk was warm, delicious, thick, heavy, and it had pretty much every other positive adjective I could think of.

I was addicted to it, and I wasn't going to deny that.

Seconds later, I noticed that Stephen was also coming inside of me. His sperm was also thick and warm, and I could feel it filling me up. I knew that, after tonight, after feeling so much pain and pleasure at the same time, I would never feel the same again.

Then, he pulled out. Both of them pulled out, in fact, leaving me alone on the floor in the hallway. Stephen had milked me dry, but there was still some milk escaping my nipples, which was to be expected. If there was something I learned about my body now that I was a hucow, it was that I never stopped making milk.

"We are leaving now, but we are going to be back for you when you are in your cell again. Don't worry – we are going to take good care of you, and we are also going to look after you. You don't need to worry about anything. This was only your first milking here with us and as you learn about how to be a hucow, everything will be resolved and then you will be sold."

At this point, my mind was dizzy and everything was a blur to me. I couldn't even understand properly what they were saying, but I knew that it was good. I couldn't help but feel excited and also a little anxious that they were going to milk me many more times in the future.

It was my dream.

The End

Thank you for reading this story. Leave your review. Your feedback helps me immensely!

TEASER: HANDCUFFED FOR BAD BEHAVIOR

Hucow Milking Story

Not the place where I wanted to be.

Not with these people looking at me.

I mean, I was in the middle of a crowd, but I was still certain that they were looking at me.

Judging me.

Someone was standing on a raised platform and speaking, but I couldn't pay any attention to his words.

I couldn't stop thinking that something had to be wrong with this. All the hucows were women and all the trainers and professors were men.

Obviously, all the hucows were going to be women, but all the teachers were men? What the hell was going on here?

They were keeping us naked in the main hall, and we couldn't do anything about it.

One peep and it would be enough to put us in their cells.

They were cold, unforgiving. I couldn't stand even thinking about those cells, and I was certain that it would never happen to me.

The teachers would never put us in one of those cells.

It didn't matter that they were all smoking hot.

They were never going to make me think that anything could ever happen between us.

Even though…

Even though the reason why I came here was simple.

I thought that I could strike gold by coming here. Thought that one of the teachers would have eyes for me, but that lasted until I realized that they were all married.

And I wasn't lying. All of them had marriage rings on their fingers, destroying all hope that I once had. So why did I even think that coming here was going to solve anything?

The truth was that it wasn't going to solve anything.

We were all here, in the main hall, and the teacher on the raised platform was speaking about what our lives here were going to be like.

It was like time was passing but wasn't at the same time.

I took a deep breath in, closed my eyes, and thought that for sure nothing else was going to happen here.

We were going to be taken to our bedrooms, they were going to lock us in there, and that was going to be it.

I was so certain of that that I wasn't even aware of what was happening around me or what my ears were hearing.

That was why I was so stunned when I noticed someone right by my side, and it wasn't one of the candidates.

It was actually a man. One of the teachers, I noticed right away. He was nothing short of stunning.

He looked just like all the other teachers, but he was also different.

Blond hair.

Stubble on his face.

Square jawline.

Full lips.

A massive, hulky body.

And eyes that looked into mine as though he could read everything I was thinking.

Even though I wasn't even trying to say anything, I felt like I was mumbling. I was so stunned that my body had frozen up. And

I was certain that he was aware of the effect he was having on me. It was why he wasn't smiling right now.

Such a devilish, evil smile, and he wasn't ashamed of it.

And I was certain that he knew how aroused he was making me feel, too.

After all, why else would he be pulling up the side of his lips like that, showing me a little of his teeth? Even though I couldn't see much, there was no denying that they were shining.

"Who are you?" I asked, hoping that he was going to be forthcoming with his answer, but knowing that he didn't have to.

He didn't say anything for the first few seconds, making me feel so anxious, and I was certain he was using that to his advantage as well.

If there was something I learned about the teachers here in Deimour College, it was that they had no boundaries when it came to taking advantage of their students.

"I'm Jason. I'm one of the teachers here in the college," he replied, not giving me any new information. Of course he wouldn't.

"I already knew that," I said, my eyes moving up and down while I felt some wetness and heat between my legs. It was impossible not to be feeling that way when he was so hot and was so incredibly close to me.

He was so close that he was making it difficult for me to breathe.

I just couldn't stop scrutinizing every part of his body.

His rippling muscles.

His bulging biceps.

His crotch.

The way his shirt showed off his abs.

And pretty much everything else. The more I looked at this man, Jason, the more I felt absolutely stunned.

And that made me feel like doing something I thought I never would.

Bad behavior.

Behaving in a way that would put me into trouble.

I knew that was a mistake, but I was still willing to go through with it until the end.

But what would be my punishment if that happened?

"Do you want something from me?" I asked and for the time being, it was like everything happening around me didn't matter anymore.

"I don't know. You tell me."

I checked him out from bottom to top again, my eyes lingering on his crotch. I didn't know if he was wearing tight boxer briefs, but his bulge was so big, and it kept on making me think about what it would be like to feel it with my fingers.

Should I do that? I didn't know, and I was soon realizing that I had to make a decision. After all, the other teacher, whose name I didn't know, was already moving away from the raised platform after speaking his lines in front of the students.

We were all going somewhere else, but I realized that I didn't have to.

After all, Jason was with me.

His eyes were staring at me.

"I think you know what I want from you, and I think you also know why you came here."

He was so sure of himself that it was maddening, and it still melted my heart.

Could I really not do what he wanted? The more time passed here, the more I realized that it was impossible not to.

Thus, without giving it a second thought, I just moved away with him somewhere else.

But we weren't going with the other teachers and the students. We were going to a separate room in Deimour College, and I couldn't wait for some sexy time with Jason.

I knew he was unbelievably hung.

SIMILAR BOOKS

BUNDLE - HUCOW PRISON

All the books of the Hucow Prison series in one single, convenient collection.

1. Hucow Prison

SERIES - FERTILE ONLY

1. Bumping the Teacher

2. Bumping the Midwife

3. Bumping the Farmhand

4. Bumping the Sinner

SERIES - HIS HERD

1. Peculiar Dairy

2. Milked by her Boyfriend

3. Menage for Milking

4. Farm Milking

5. Fertile for my Farmers

ABOUT THE AUTHOR

Leandra Camilli's obsession? Writing dirty, steamy stories that make her readers drool. She loves her Alpha males, hucows, sissies, and futas. If you're looking for those kinds of books, look no further.

With a cup of coffee on her table and warm socks on, she writes almost every day. Leandra Camilli has featured in several top 100 categories in the store, and she publishes weekly.